This innovative project encourages children ages seven to twelve to become "emotional ecologists," determined to become more responsible as they grow up and leave a better world for those who follow them, and who will in turn help a new generation develop.

It is an open invitation to reflect, debate, develop creatively, and share experiences that allow personal improvement. Only if we are conscious that something is of value will we defend it, take care of it, respect it, and then watch it grow.

We hope you enjoy this innovative concept as you embark on an exciting exploration of yourself and the world around you!

To Zulma and the whole generation of CAPA children

HOW DOES THIS BOOK WORK?

The content is purposefully open, leaving space for mentors and teachers to enrich the activities and ideas in their own way.

The book consists of five chapters that follow the same structure:

Each chapter begins with a double page of illustrations and poses three questions. These three questions are reflected in the illustrations, sparking debate and an exchange of opinions on the chapter's theme. This encourages learners to "see" and "read" much more than what appears on the printed page.

Presenting a parallel or analogy between the world around us and our inner world, this double-page spread uses text and illustrations to examine what we call "emotional ecology." This approach will help us to better understand what is happening inside us, what the causes are, and any consequences that may arise.

These two pages encompass both environmental education and emotional education; one concept complements and enriches the other, allowing us to develop and better understand both of them.

Now that we have identified what happens inside us and what the consequences may be, the **third double-page spread encourages us to think** about how we can act differently and better adapt ourselves. Full-page illustrations again serve as an invitation to participate and ask questions, further engaging students and proposing possible tools and solutions that will help them realize their objectives.

The six proposals put forward in each chapter (through activities, stories, games, or hypothetical situations) **allow us to work on the skills we need to overcome the obstacles identified therein**, helping us to become stronger and more emotionally ecological.

A brief guide for mentors and teachers accompanies each scenario, allowing them to tailor the activities to a group or situation.

Each exercise follows the same structure and consists of four distinct sections: an objective that addresses the scenario; an explanation of the scenario; reflections on the exercise; and conclusions that can be drawn for further investigation.

If you like the proposed scenarios, we invite you without further ado to let go of everything weighing you down and learn to fly using renewable, sustainable, and ecological energy, to produce and store emotional vitamins, and surround yourself with good friends and happiness, and avoid "prickles."

SUMMARY

LEARNING TO FLY

- WHY DO KITES FLY?
- IS IT POSSIBLE TO FLY WITHOUT WINGS?
- DID YOU KNOW THAT EMOTIONAL ENERGY GIVES US THE STRENGTH TO "TAKE OFF"?

Wings are limbs that only insects, birds, and bats possess. They are normally used to fly, although not all animals that have wings are able to take to the air; some, like the emu, penguin, kiwi, chicken, and ostrich, have wings but cannot fly. Other creatures have membranes between their legs and bodies or their fingers and toes (such as the flying frog) but can only glide short distances. Did you know that some tiny spiders produce their own silk parachutes with the same material they use to spin their webs? The wind lifts these parachutes, moving the spiders around.

Did you know that the flying squirrel has folds of skin stretched along its body that act as sails, catching in the wind and allowing it to glide from tree to tree? It could even glide across a soccer field!

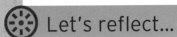

Let's reflect...

- How could having wings help you?

- Why do you think we use the expression, "I'm walking on air" when we are happy?

- Why is it that some winged animals can't fly? Are they too heavy, or are their wings too small in relation to their bodies? Perhaps they are afraid to fly and feel safer on the ground? What do you think?

Human beings don't have wings. We can run, jump, dance, walk, and move from side to side, but never far from ground level. However, we can fly in our imagination, invent things, and dream. Furthermore, our intelligence has allowed us to create flying vehicles (aircraft, helicopters, hang gliders) that imitate birds. When someone says, "I feel light, as if I am flying," it means they feel happy and full of energy.

Do you know what gives us wings? What gives us the confidence to do what we think is important? By contrast, what can tether our dreams and hold back our imagination?

"Flying" means we acquire the confidence we need to explore and become CAPAs: Creative, autonomous, peaceful, and affectionate.

☀ Let's reflect...

- What can we create during our lives?
- Who do we love?
- Do we look for peaceful solutions to our problems?
- What does the word autonomous mean? What can we do on our own, and what do we need the help of others to achieve?
- Are we able to work towards improving our own self-worth?

WOULD YOU LIKE TO BECOME A PERSON WHO IS ABLE TO **MAKE YOUR DREAMS BECOME REALITY?**

WOULD YOU LIKE TO HAVE **ENOUGH CONFIDENCE IN YOURSELF** TO TAKE WORTHWHILE RISKS?

MY CAPA KITE

⚙ Objective:

To work in CAPA's four dimensions (creative, autonomous, peaceful, and affectionate) toward emotional ecology. To become aware of strengths and areas that require improvement.

Activity:

Give each student a piece of paper with a picture of a small kite and the following commentary from Erma Bombeck printed on it:

"Children are like kites. You spend years trying to get them off the ground. You run with them until you are both breathless. They crash . . . they hit the roof . . . you patch, comfort, and assure them that someday they will fly. Finally, they are airborne. They need more string, and you keep letting it out. They tug, and with each twist of the twine, there is sadness that goes with joy. The kite becomes more distant, and you know it won't be long before that beautiful creature will snap the lifeline that binds you together and will soar as it is meant to soar . . . free and alone. Only then do you know that you have done your job."

In this exercise, each child will use the picture to create his own kite, customizing it with drawings and colors. One of the four CAPA initials must be written in each of the kite's four segments: the "C" of creative, "A" of autonomous, "P" of peaceful, and "A" of affectionate.

The kites are then hung from the classroom ceiling with nylon thread. Each kite will be inspected in turn for the richness of its diversity and the uniqueness of its beauty. Finally, the class will work together to create a much larger kite to further decorate the classroom, revisiting the concept of working toward becoming CAPAs.

⚙ Reflecting on this exercise

- What would you say is the purpose of a kite?
- What can stop a kite from flying?
- If you were a kite, what would your wind be?
- Which three things can you do to improve each of your CAPA qualities, becoming more creative, affectionate, peaceful, and autonomous?
- What do you think is fundamental to maintain balance between all four segments?

⚙ Conclusions and other considerations

A "CAPA" is:

- **Creative:** Flexible, able to look at things from different points of view, dream, imagine, be constructive.
- **Autonomous:** Builds healthy relationships, is self-confident, critical, maintains emotional hygiene daily, knows how to be alone but also enjoys the company of others.
- **Peaceful:** Resolves problems without attacking or injuring others or themselves. Works toward a peaceful culture and knows how to control different emotions.
- **Affectionate:** Approachable, responsible, respectful, engaging, a communicator, tender, patient, nurtures happiness.

THE PERSON I AM

⚙ Objective:

Learn to describe yourself by selecting the essential characteristics that define us all.

Activity:

Each participant writes a sentence (six words maximum) on a card describing the type of person they are. The mentor passes a box around the group and the cards are all placed inside. Once all the cards have been collected, the mentor puts them on the classroom wall, with an accompanying number for identification.

In this exercise each participant must read the descriptions on the cards and identify which members of the group have written them.

Then they take turns guessing which card belongs to who, and why. Finally, each member of the group confirms which card is theirs and explains why they think the sentence they have written describes them.

⚙ Reflecting on this exercise

- Was it difficult to describe yourself in only six words?
- If you could choose just three of the six words you used to describe yourself, which would they be?
- Did other group members easily guess which card you had written?
- Were there many differences between how you see yourself and how others see you?
- Could you correctly identify most of the group members?
- Would you say that you know each other well?

⚙ Conclusions and other considerations

Others may see us in a very different way from how we see ourselves. How we perceive ourselves does not always coincide with how other people see us.

Sometimes we only show a small part of who we are, and do not allow others to access the treasure inside us. But what good is being rich without being able to enjoy it? It is important to show the best of ourselves to others, thus improving our personal relationships.

MY LOVE LETTER

☀ Objective:

To become aware of how important it is to love ourselves and be able to love others. To dedicate time to recognizing that we deserve to be loved and learning how to express our love.

Activity:

Read the following instructions out loud to the group:

You are going to write a letter to a person you have known for several years. It should be someone who has always been close to you, although sometimes it doesn't appear that way and you have felt alone. It should be someone who worries about you, takes care of you, and will never leave you. This very special person deserves your recognition, and so we suggest you write them a 'love letter' describing everything you value about them: acknowledge their best qualities and remind them of the best moments you have shared together, as well as the times you have been sad and cried because you missed them. It is very important that you take the opportunity to get to know them better every day and express how lucky you feel to share your life with them.

Give each group member a sheet of paper, an envelope, tape, and a piece of paper with the name of the person who will receive the letter. Write on the paper: "You are this person."

Each participant writes the letter in silence and then places it inside the envelope. It must be fully addressed, sealed with the tape, and given to the mentor who will mail the letters one at a time, over several days. In this way the letter writers will not know when their letters will be delivered, heightening expectation.

In a future session the group can comment on how their loved ones felt when they received their letters.

❀ Reflecting on this exercise

- How did you feel as you were writing this letter? Was it difficult?

- Do you think the addressee was pleased to receive it?

- Have you ever said to yourself what you wrote in the letter? Why?

- What new characteristics have you discovered in yourself?

- Why do you think you deserve to be loved?

- How often do you think you should write a love letter like this one?

❀ Conclusions and other considerations

Love is a white light composed of a spectrum of brilliant colors: green for hope, yellow for happiness, tender pink, serene blue, passionate red, etc. When this love-light shines on a receptive person, it is reflected in them and the colors appear to them as a rainbow. But if your love-light shines on someone who does not respond, it can stay hidden . . . and the darkness is absolute.

It is important to work on our responsiveness, polishing and buffing our interior mirror every day, so that the light of our love reflects in all colors and we are able to love those around us.

ALONE OR ACCOMPANIED?

⚙ Objective:

It is important to note that being autonomous is not the same as being individualistic, nor is being accompanied the same as depending on someone else. Likewise, receiving suggestions is not the same as being given orders.

Activity:

Arrange the chairs and tables to form a labyrinth or circuit, complete with obstacles, dead ends, junctions, and objects attached to the floor and ceiling (such as balloons or strips of paper forming a spider's web). Mentors should use their imagination! Recorded noises, alarms, and sounds of the natural world can also be deployed.

Create both a starting point and a finishing point, where the collective CAPA kite will be located. Participants must navigate the circuit blindfolded. When they arrive at the kite, they will have reached the end of their journey. This is the first stage of the exercise.

The participants leave the classroom while the circuit is modified. This time two group members participate: one enters the circuit blindfolded while the other guides them with verbal instructions. Under no circumstances should the guide touch or accompany their partner along the way.

In the last phase of this exercise, the circuit is again rearranged. One participant enters blindfolded while a guide is permitted to accompany them, giving directions through minimum physical contact. The guide is forbidden to speak.

Finally, the participants take a few minutes to draw their own conclusions about each stage of the exercise. Further debate should explore the emotions they experienced.

⚙ Reflecting on this exercise

- How did you feel when you took part in this activity on your own? What kind of emotions did you experience? Did you meet your objective? Or did you hurt yourself? Did you remove your blindfold at any time?

- How did you feel when you were following your partner's instructions? Did they inspire confidence or make you feel insecure? Why? Was it easier or more difficult to complete the circuit alone or with a guide? Why?

- What did you experience during the last stage of this exercise? What emotions did you feel on physical contact with your companion? Did it make you feel uncomfortable or generate a feeling of well-being?

- Can you tell the difference between autonomy and individualism, and between dependence and accompaniment?

⚙ Conclusions and other considerations

While we depend on others when we are alone, we cannot acquire from them what we need to feel healthy and balanced. We can feel lost without that person to depend on and ready to do whatever it takes so that they do not abandon us.

An autonomous person values the company and support of others but works alone to achieve their objectives without waiting for others to solve the problems in their life.

An individualistic person believes that they can deal with their problems alone, and does not value others' help.

Accompanying another means respecting their personal rhythm and 'weather.' We can make suggestions and give indicators but should never dictate or give orders.

Autonomy represents an important section of our 'emotional wings,' and we must cultivate it every day so that we do not have problems in our relationships with others.

THE NOBEL PEACE PRIZE

✿ Objective:

Research public figures that have made contributions to world peace. Analyze their contributions, finding clear examples of their actions that we can adapt to cultivate peace in our day-to-day lives.

Activity:

Search the Internet for a list of different Nobel Prize winners, from its inception up to the present day.

Form three working groups to further research this list. Each group should choose one prizewinner. Their task is then to:

- Investigate the prizewinner's biography.
- Highlight three personal qualities recognized in this biography.
- Distinguish what qualified them to receive the award.
- All working groups should consider the following question: How would the world have been different if their chosen prizewinner had never been born?
- Finally, each group member selects one of their own aspects or characteristics that they would like to work at within themselves, enhancing their 'peaceful' CAPA segment.

When each group has completed its research they present their findings to the other groups, justifying their choice of prizewinner. Compare the different profiles of all of the candidates and the contributions they have made. Try to reach a consensus about which candidate has contributed most to the cause of world peace.

✿ Reflecting on this exercise

- Did you know what the Nobel prizes are? What is their purpose?

- Do you think that there are people who have not received awards for their contributions to world peace but do magnificent work in this area? Can you think of any names?

- Do you believe that we are at war with our own planet?

- Do you think it is possible to sign a peace treaty with the Earth? What might that treaty be like?

- And you . . . are you at peace or at war with yourself?

- Which three actions in particular could you collaborate in to help promote a peaceful culture?

✿ Conclusions and other considerations

A peaceful person does not trespass into the territory of others or interfere in their lives, and knows how to maintain an appropriate distance. They are also able to show respect to those around them, avoiding emotional pollution and working to maintain an acceptable level of self-control.

A peaceful person focuses on improving as a person instead of expecting change in others, disposes of their everyday toxic emotional waste and uses 'bridge words' rather than hurtful 'dart words.'

The peaceful person is able to recognize their mistakes and does not avoid conflict but resolves it with calm and inner peace.

ALL KINDS OF WINGS

✿ Objective:

Consider the huge diversity of creatures that inhabit this planet. Be aware that a particular quality or characteristic that someone possesses is not necessarily useful to them.

Activity:

Form teams within the group. Each team must research five different types of winged animals (whether they are able to fly or not), draw pictures of them, and tell the others about their findings.

Each team prepares a set of rectangular cards, then draws or glues an image of a wing belonging to one of the animals that they have researched. On another card they write the type of animal.

Shuffle the picture and name cards together, and invite all of the teams to play. There are many different games that can be played with these cards; for example: pair up the names with their corresponding wings (memory game), or deal out the cards and use them as dominoes (the first player to empty their hand is the winner).

The second part of the exercise uses the backs of the cards. Choose a quality that can boost self-reliance (e.g., courage) and write it on the back of the picture cards. On the corresponding name cards, where the names of the winged animal appears, write phrases that show situations where this quality can be applied (e.g., "tell the truth").

Once the cards have been prepared the group can again play pairs or dominoes.

✿ Reflecting on this exercise

- Which qualities would you like to possess?

- Which two things can you do to become more confident and courageous?

- When you are frightened, what do you say to yourself to lift your spirits?

- Now that you know more about different winged creatures, would you like to have any of their characteristics? Why?

- Have you ever had the feeling that your parents or friends are pushing you to 'jump,' so that you can spread your wings and learn to fly?

✿ Conclusions and other considerations

Some adults have immense wings like eagles, allowing them to fly high up into the sky and traverse huge distances. They are able to see things that go unnoticed by others, who are closer to the ground. Others have wings more like the butterfly: beautiful and delicate. These people fly closer to the ground and pollinate flowers across the countryside. But is it better to be an eagle than a butterfly? No. Both are perfect just as they are. There are other people who have wings but have not used them for a very long time and cannot fly any more, like chickens.

Human beings have qualities that, like wings, will help us to grow if we use them well. It is simply a matter of training every day.

ENERGIES

- WHICH SOURCES OF ENERGY DOES THE EARTH HAVE?
- WHERE CAN WE FIND THE ENERGY THAT WE NEED TO SURVIVE?
- DID YOU KNOW THAT THERE ARE ALSO SOURCES OF EMOTIONAL ENERGY?

?

Energy moves us. There is hidden energy in the air around us: In the water, the sun, buried in the earth, and inside each and every cell of our bodies.

Some sources of energy are contaminants (such as coal, oil, and nuclear energy) that damage our ecosystem, destroy forests, pollute our rivers, seas, and the air that we breathe, and cause sickness and disease. However, other energy sources are ecological, clean and renewable (such as solar, biomass, hydraulic, tidal, geothermal, and wind power); it is vital that we learn to harness them effectively so that they are useful to us.

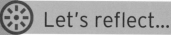 Let's reflect...

- Did you know that windmills were invented 3,000 years ago?

- Did you know that the sun emits 4,000 times more energy each year than we consume?

- And that water wheels, invented thousands of years ago, were used extensively in the Middle Ages?

- Do you know which clean energy sources are available to us and what their advantages are?

Some emotions radiate enormous amounts of energy. For example, happiness and love are creative energies, helping to improve the world by making it a brighter and more brilliant place. Both of these energies are renewable (they are not depleted even after they are expressed), sustainable (can be maintained and increased without draining the person who uses them), and ecological (improve global balance and promote healthy living).

Contrarily, the energy emitted by anger can be dangerous if it is out of control; it can turn us into destructive and malicious individuals. This is why it is essential that we learn to channel and correctly orient this classification of 'dangerous' energies, managing them more ecologically (instead of breaking, we can build; rather than scream, sing; instead of fighting, exercise; rather than complain, look for solutions, etc.).

When we do something powered by a 'contaminated' emotional energy source we feel tired, discouraged, frustrated, sad, and dissatisfied. But when we plug into a source of ecological energy we feel cheerful, motivated, happy, and at peace.

⚙ Let's reflect...

- What kind of emotional energy would you prefer to use?

- What happens to you when you are obligated to do something, rather than acting out of happiness and love?

19

IS IT A CLEAN, RENEWABLE, SUSTAINABLE, AND ECOLOGICAL SOURCE, OR A **CONTAMINATED SOURCE?**

IDEAS
FOR THE BEST USE OF EMOTIONAL ENERGY

ON A ROCK OR IN THE SAND?

⚙ Objective:
Consider that every one of us must choose how we treat others. Learn how important it is to know how to forgive.

Narrative:

Two friends, Victor and Roberto, are traveling across the desert when they start to argue. Victor slaps Roberto hard. Roberto, clearly offended but without saying a word, bends down and writes in the sand with his finger: "Today my best friend slapped me hard in the face." They continue on their way until they reach an oasis, where they decide to go for a swim. Roberto struggles and begins to drown. Victor, realizing that his friend is in trouble, pulls him from the water, rescuing him. When Roberto recovers he takes up a stylet and starts to scratch something onto a nearby boulder. When he has finished, it reads: "Today my best friend saved my life."

Intrigued, Victor asked him:

"Why did you write in the sand when I hurt you but now you are writing on rock?"

A smiling Roberto replied:

"When a good friend does something to offend us we should write their wrongdoings in the sand as the wind of forgive and forget will soon blow the grains away. However, when a good friend helps us out we should record it in stone, so that no wind is able to erase it."

⚙ Reflecting on this narrative

- Which type of emotional energy was Roberto connecting to?
- What do you think could have happened if he had taken offense and become angry?
- Do you think that sometimes silence is the best strategy?
- Which memories stay with you most clearly: pleasant or unpleasant? Why?
- Which unpleasant memories and moments when you have been offended would you like the wind of forgive and forget to blow away?
- Which precious moments would you like to have engraved forever in the memory of your heart?
- What must you do to forgive someone? What should you do if someone asks your forgiveness?

⚙ Conclusions and other considerations

Anger, offense, resentment, bitterness, and revenge are poisonous and toxic emotional sources. When we plug into them we increase levels of suffering in the world, contribute to destruction and chaos, and invite unhappiness into our lives.

Forgiveness, forgetting that we have been offended, friendship, and generosity are clean, renewable, and sustainable sources of emotional energy. On connecting with them our lives will improve and we will contribute to a more peaceful and loving world.

POSITIVE OR NEGATIVE OUTLOOK?

✲ Objective:

To become aware that different things will happen to us depending on the source of energy that we connect to.

Narrative:

Two frogs fall into an enormous bucket of cream. One says to the other:

"We're doomed! Better that we just give up now."

"Keep swimming," the other replied. "We'll get out of this one way or another."

"But it's pointless!" cried the first frog. "This cream is too thick to swim in, too soft to jump on, and too slippery to crawl out of. As I'm going to die anyway, better sooner than later."

And letting himself sink beneath the surface, he drowned. However, his friend refused to give up and continued swimming. Later he woke up on top of a block of butter that he had formed by beating the cream as he swam. And there he stayed, grinning as he ate the flies that were converging from every direction.

⦂ Reflecting on this narrative

- What do you think about how the first frog reacted to the situation? What kind of emotions was he experiencing when he decided he was doomed? What did he end up doing?

- What do you believe the second frog was thinking? Which emotions do you believe he was experiencing as he made his decision to survive? How did he react?

- What happened to each of the frogs? Why do you think that things turned out the way they did?

- Which frog is more like you? Why?

- What have you learned from this narrative?

⦂ Conclusions and other considerations

The way we think raises certain emotions in us.

If we think that we can't do something, or that something bad is going to happen if we do, we will feel disheartened, sad, fearful, or panicky; it is therefore probable that things are going to end badly.

If, on the other hand, we think that even if something is difficult we can work hard to ensure that it turns out for the best, this will fill us with the courage, motivation, and hope that we need to move forward.

This positive outlook is an extremely valuable and useful source of energy that we have at our disposal. It could be compared to wearing special glasses that allow us to assess a situation that may appear unsolvable from another point of view.

23

SHALL WE MAKE A KOLAM?

⚙ Objective:

Learn to begin the day connected to grateful energy. This feeling comes from being conscious that every day is a gift and that we do our best to enjoy everything that it offers us.

Activity:

Read the following narrative out loud:

Many Hindu villagers begin their day by sweeping the floor of their porch. They clean it and flatten it (if it is soil) until it is as good as new. At the moment the Sun appears on the horizon they begin their daily ritual: using white or colored chalks, different-colored soils, paint, the leaves of different plants, sticks, or any other materials that they have at hand, they use their inspiration to create a picture on the ground (sometimes based on geometric shapes, floral designs, circles, spirals, etc.). While they work they meditate, saying:

"Hello, newborn Sun. Thank you for rising. Thank you life, for the start of this new day. I am grateful to be here and to be alive. I welcome everything that today will bring: What I will learn, visitors to my home, happy things, and sad things alike. I am grateful for these gifts."

This is how they start their day, conscious that life is a gift. Their picture will welcome visitors to their homes. The following day, as the Sun rises again, they will erase the pictures that they so painstakingly and creatively formed. It doesn't matter to them if it was magnificent or marvelous, or the amount of time they invested in its creation. It is yesterday's picture and is no longer relevant. Yesterday has passed. Today is another day. There is no value to living in the past. Every day has its own picture.

Then give each participant an A3 sheet of paper or cardboard, placing it in on the ground at their feet. Their task is to create a Kolam that will welcome a new day in their lives and to be grateful for the gifts that it will bring. Place paints, markers, and other materials that they can use in the middle of the classroom.

⚙ Reflecting on this exercise

- Why not search for different types of Kolam on the internet?
- What do you think about this Hindu tradition?
- How do you think that connecting to gratitude could improve your day?
- How would you define this feeling?
- Which things in life cheer you up?
- Do you often give thanks?
- How do you respond when someone thanks you for something?
- Are you able to share with the group how you felt when you were creating your Kolam?

⚙ Conclusions and other considerations

Appreciation is the expression of a feeling of gratitude. Cultivating this emotion yields healthy fruit and almost immediate results, as we are connected to a source of emotional energy.

When we are generous we feel fortunate and happy, triggering a boomerang effect - meaning that our generosity is appreciated and returned to us.

Are we aware of the gifts we receive? Gratitude changes the world for the better. It is a great self-motivator, bringing people together and healing and repairing emotional injuries.

We can find something to be grateful for even in the worst of situations.

GOOD NEWS

⊛ Objective:

Learn to find positives even in negative situations.

Activity:

Encourage the group to collect newspaper articles about world events that occur over the course of one week.

Issue the following instructions to the group:

You are going to form three teams of emotionally ecological journalists. Your mission is to create a newspaper containing only positive real-life news articles. To do so you must work as a team, searching (for about half an hour) for articles in newspapers which may be deemed positive. Cut them out before classifying them by sections or themes.

Once you have finished, start to create your publication. You will be provided with A3 sheets of paper, scissors, glue, felt-tip pens, etc.

Important: Indicate which newspaper you have taken the cutting from and the date that it was published underneath each article.

Once you have finished, work together to write an editorial presenting your publication and a list of news that the reader will find within its pages.

Finally, each group should present their publication to the class as a whole and highlight the three best news stories that they have uncovered.

⊛ Reflecting on this exercise

- Do you think that a newspaper reporting only good news would be popular? Do you think that people would buy it? Why?

- Did it prove difficult to find positive news articles over the week?

- Do you think that the positive things that happen around the world are worth reporting?

- Would you approve of a 'positive news newspaper' about yourself? Why not design a front page that highlights what is important to you right now?

- How do you think that you can advocate positive ideas, thoughts, emotions, and facts to those around you?

- What kind of emotions does bad news connect us to?

- What kind of emotions does good news connect us to?

⊛ Conclusions and other considerations

There is much beauty but also ugliness in the world. Good things and bad things happen, which can be both creative and destructive.

The world is the way it is because we are like we are. If we don't like something about it, we should try to change it.

Destruction and evil often create a lot of noise; that is why they may seem to dominate the world. However, goodness, beauty, and love are always present; often in silence, but quietly doing their jobs day in and day out. It is important to recognize this and join forces with them.

We can all work together to promote goodness and give a voice to the good people who work quietly every day to make the world a better place. We must learn to recognize and pass on good news.

HAPPY JELLY

⚙ Objective:

To be conscious that when great things happen in our life, it is important to preserve them as emotional memories. When things do not go so well for us, we can use these memories to 'nourish' ourselves.

Activity:

Each participant must bring to class a recycled glass jar, complete with its metal lid. Prepare for this activity by leaving small, rectangular pieces of colored paper, felt-tip pens, patterned fabrics, labels, and ribbons around the classroom.

Each child must first decide which type of conserve they would like to prepare (happy jelly, precious moments jelly, fun experiences jelly, grateful jelly, best-of-myself jelly, etc.). They then design a label for their jelly bearing their name, the date, and the phrase "No emotional best before date." They could make a second label for the back of the jar, listing their jelly's ingredients and conditions of use.

Once the jar is labeled, each participant writes their most pleasurable moments, memories etc., on the pieces of colored paper and places them in the jar. The lid is fitted, covered with a piece of fabric, and tied with a ribbon.

Finally each participant tells the other group members what kind of jelly they made and shows it to all of them.

⚙ Reflecting on this exercise

- How did you feel as you made your pot of jelly?

- Was it difficult for you to think of pleasant memories, people, and situations?

- Do you think that you could make 'emotional jellies' to give to other people? Or how about a 'what-I-like-about-you jelly'?

- How would you feel if someone gave you a similar gift?

- Do you think that other people would like to receive a similar gift?

- What do think about the whole group making a huge 'best-moments-of-this-course jelly'?

⚙ Conclusions and other considerations

Emotional vitamins are reserves of fond memories and vivid situations that we have stored in our emotional memory. They can give us a feeling of security and energy and console us in difficult situations and crises.

What kind of emotional vitamins do we have at our disposal? There are many: hugs, smiles, laughter, kisses, grace, positive reinforcement, caresses, tender words, fond reminders, special moments, shared happiness, etc. Are these things that you give often? Do you know how to receive them when they are given to you?

Poets for a Day

⊛ Objective:

To be conscious of the small, everyday pleasures that we have at our disposal. While they do not involve spending money, they are valuable because they provide and generate well-being.

Activity:

Give each student a copy of Bertolt Brecht's *Pleasures* and read it out loud:

First look from morning's window
the rediscovered book
fascinated faces
snow, the change of the seasons
the newspaper, the dog, dialectics
showering, swimming, old music
comfortable shoes
comprehension
new music
writing, planting, traveling, singing
being friendly.

The mentor states that it is very important for each person to identify what is pleasurable and satisfying to them. These things must be readily available and not cost any money or depend on someone else's initiative (for example, they can't just say "Rosa says that she loves me," or "my friends have invited me to cinema," as both depend on decisions made by others).

Once this is understood, each participant should pen their own poem entitled 'Pleasures,' in which they should include all the things that cheer and brighten up their lives.

When they are finished, each participant should read their poem out loud to the rest of the group. They could also compose a list of all the good and pleasant things that they have at their disposal.

⊛ Reflecting on this exercise

- How did you feel after writing your poem?

- Could you have added to the list of pleasurable things that you have at your disposal?

- What do you think about pinning your poem to a notice board or wall at home and adding new pleasurable things as they happen to you?

- What type of emotional sources do you think that you connected to during this exercise?

- What is the difference between 'price' and 'value'?

- Can you find examples of things that are of great value to you but cost little, and things that are expensive but have minimal value to you?

⊛ Conclusions and other considerations

Self-motivation is the ability to connect yourself to sources of emotional energy that move you to action. It is one of the competencies that emotionally intelligent people possess.

Life is full of gifts if we pay attention: Walking along the beach barefoot, listening to the music that the rain makes, splashing in a puddle, or letting the sun warm our faces . . . everyone has their own small pleasures that bring them energy and equilibrium.

It is important to allow ourselves special moments such as these because we can only provide comfort to others if we are comfortable with ourselves.

27

HEDGEHOGS AND OTHER PRICKLY CREATURES

- Do you know of any animals or plants that are prickly?
- What do you think THORNS, SPIKES, AND SPINES are useful for?
- Do you have any "PRICKLES"?

?

29

Some animals and plants are protected from attacks so others cannot harm them. There are many different defensive mechanisms (for example, sea urchins are protected with barbs, scorpion fish with spines, the stingray and bees with a sting, and cats with retractable claws). Their basic objective is survival. Some of them, like sea urchins, have these defenses permanently on display. Others, like cats, attack only if they are threatened but also know how to enjoy a caress.

✳ Let's reflect...

- Did you know that the African bee is also known as 'the killer bee' because of its highly aggressive nature? Consider that it takes an African bee 20-25 minutes to 'calm down' when it is 'irritated,' while it only takes a European bee 2-3 minutes!

  The causes of their anger are varied: From the noise produced by a motor engine to the smell of gasoline, their use by beekeepers, or the movement of people or animals.

- Did you know that hedgehogs can have between 500 and 700 spines on their backs? As soon as they feel threatened or become angry, they raise these spines to protect themselves. Spines additionally serve to cushion blows or dig into any predator.

- Did you know that a stingray is armed with a powerful sting that secretes poison?

- Which other natural defensive systems can you think of?

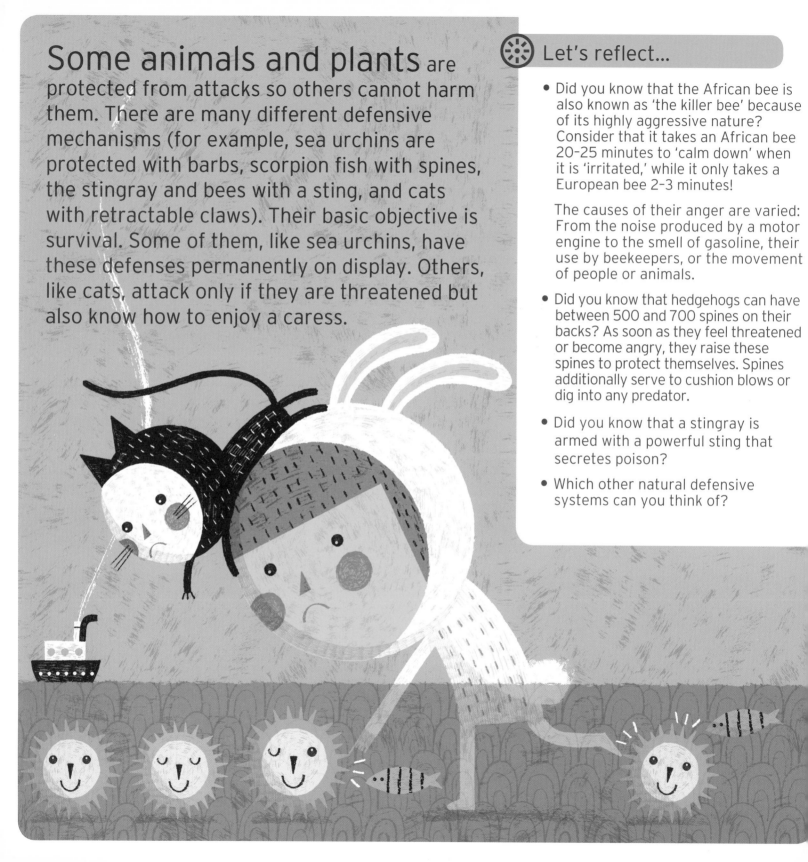

One of our main responsibilities as we learn to take care of ourselves is to avoid or protect ourselves from danger. If a situation arises where this is impossible, we must learn to defend ourselves without injuring others.

We have many protective resources, such as: Self-knowledge, emotional self-control, our ability to connect to emotionally clean energies, learning how to best choose our friends, knowing which environments to avoid because they can harm us, and working to create positive emotional weather wherever we go.

Our defensive capabilities include: Learning when to say no, carefully choosing our words, learning to give positive criticism, knowing our limits, and knowing when to keep silent.

However, we should avoid going on the attack, using destructive criticism, insults, disrespectful behavior, lies, verbal and physical aggression, rumors to discredit others, etc.

While our defensive and protective capabilities are essential, we should not use them aggressively as they will only cause suffering and destruction.

 Let's reflect...

- Do you have spines? Are they always raised?

- If not, which situations and which type of person makes you raise them?

WHY DO YOU **SOMETIMES FOLLOW** THE DANGEROUS PATH OF ATTACKING OR DAMAGING OTHERS?

NOT JUST PRICKLES

⊛ Objective:
Learn that self-defense mechanisms are not negative, but an essential part of taking care of ourselves.

Narrative:

The cactus is humble, but not submissive. It can grow where no other plant is able to grow. It does not complain if it is thirsty or sunburned or if the wind pulls it from a cliff or buries it in the dry desert sand. When it rains it stores water for drier times ahead. Its flowers bloom in both good weather and bad. It protects itself from danger but does not harm any other plant. It is perfectly adapted to almost every environment. In Mexico there is a cactus that only blooms at night once every hundred years. Isn't that wonderful?

Furthermore the cactus can be used to produce balms and medicines that we humans can use to cure our ailments. It is a plant of patience and loneliness, love and madness, beauty and ugliness, toughness and frailty.

⊛ Reflecting on this narrative

- What does it mean to be humble?

- What is the difference between 'humility' and 'submission'?

- What do cacti do with rainwater?

- What do you think of the fact that the cactus blooms in both good times and bad?

- What purpose do you think its spines serve? What are cacti protected from?

- Can you find information about what cacti are useful for?

⊛ Conclusions and other considerations

The word humility derives from 'humus,' meaning 'soil.' Humility is an essential characteristic that we must all develop. A humble person is aware of their qualities but does not flaunt them and knows how to use their resources without harming others.

Like cacti, we must learn to protect ourselves from everything that can harm us without going on the attack, and learn to avoid aggression before it occurs.

It is also important that we learn to adapt to the different emotional weather that we experience.

To survive through difficult times it is important that we, like the cactus, maintain 'good water reserves.' In this case water represents our personal resources, or those qualities that we can develop and improve to help us through the more difficult moments in our lives.

OUR OWN PERSONAL HEDGEHOG

Objective:

To recognize the proper way to approach each person, avoid 'hurting,' 'being hurt,' and learning to respectfully relate to others.

Activity:

Distribute copies of this text, based on a narrative by Schopenhauer, so that all group members can read it through carefully:

One dark, cold night a group of hedgehogs discovered that if they huddled together they could keep warm. But as they moved closer and closer together, they prickled each other with their quills and jumped back, startled. As they moved further apart they missed each other's warmth, but at the same time they were afraid of getting hurt. After a short while they overcame their fear and huddled together, but they prickled each other again. And so this went on until they found the ideal proximity to each other: Close enough to be cozy but far enough away to not cause each other harm.

Each student then crafts their own hedgehog from plasticine or fast-drying clay, painting and adding eyes before using a few cocktail sticks to represent its spines. For the second part of this exercise each participant identifies the things that make them sprout or raise their own 'defensive spines,' writing them on post-its and attaching them to individual cocktail sticks/spines.

To complete this exercise each individual explains to the rest of the group which situations or people cause them to 'raise their defenses.

Reflecting on this exercise

- Why do hedgehogs have spines?
- What advantages do they have and what problems can they cause?
- What strategy did the hedgehogs use to stay warm and fall asleep?
- Have you ever felt pain as someone has prickled you?
- Do you let others prickle you often? Why?
- Do you sometimes prickle others with your spines?
- How do you think that we can control our personal hedgehog's spines?
- Can you think of any examples of both 'aggressive' and 'protective' prickles?

Conclusions and other considerations

It is very important to maintain the correct distance from each person. This will permit us to achieve a balanced proximity to them. In some cases the distance will be smaller, and we let people get close enough to touch us (such as people who love us and friends who do not 'prickle' us). In other cases we should try to keep our distance with our spines raised until we feel enough confidence to let them into our hearts.

PRICKLES FOR ALL TASTES!

✱ Objective:

Observe the defense/protection systems that different species have evolved to survive in hazardous environments and see if you can find any parallels with human behavior.

Activity:

Form groups, whose mission is to investigate different mediums of defense and/or protection possessed by plants, land animals, marine creatures, and insects.

Search and document resources over the course of a week, including at least four pictures of different 'prickles' (spines, quills, stings, etc.).

Each species should be represented in a montage on a piece of card, and include the following information: species name, which terrain it inhabits, which defensive system it possesses and when it uses it, as well as any other interesting observations.

Once the montage is finished each group presents their findings to the rest of the class, identifying similarities between these creatures and human beings.

✱ Reflecting on this exercise

- In which 'kingdom' did you find more examples of prickles: animal or vegetable?

- Which creature received the most attention from the group?

- Did you find differences between mechanisms that protect and those that are used to actively attack?

- And as human beings do we sometimes use similar mechanisms?

- Are any mechanisms that include spines, stings, or quills absolutely necessary?

- What is the most important thing that you learned during this exercise?

✱ Conclusions and other considerations

Sometimes the words of others can dig into us like a 'sting.' On other occasions we can't get close to someone because their 'spines' are always raised (they might have been badly hurt by another person); it is important that we are patient with them, nurture their confidence, and maintain a comfortable distance until they are ready to let us approach them.

If two people are to properly relate to each other, they need to share mutual trust. We will use our prickles less and less as we learn to engage and talk together.

Fortunately we are not trees, nor animals, nor insects . . . we can use our powers of reason and communication to grow closer to someone without getting hurt.

WHAT WOULD HAPPEN IF. . . ?

Objective:

To be aware that not maintaining the correct distance from someone can have catastrophic consequences.

Activity:

Form groups that should find at least 10 examples where not respecting the 'correct distance' from someone has caused damage, accidents, or catastrophes. Distribute a worksheet with the following examples, which participants should address and then supplement until they arrive at the requisite 10:

What would happen if...?

- A planet left its orbit.

- The Earth was 10 times closer to or further away from the Sun.
- One rail on a railway track decided to move closer to the other.
- A driver did not respect the safety distance between themselves and the car in front.

If possible, each example should be documented with further information.

Each group then presents their findings to the rest of the class.

Reflecting on this exercise

- What does the word 'chaos' mean to you? How about 'cosmos'?

- Do you think that orderliness is important in our lives? Is it important in society too?

- Can we do whatever we want, whenever we want to without any consequences?

- Which 'weapons' does society use to enforce certain laws and standards?

- What would happen if there was suddenly no form of control (police, fines, judges, or courtrooms)?

- Do you agree with the assertion that you cannot do exactly as you like when you are with other people?

- Do you think that you should also respect 'correct distances' at home?

- Can you imagine what would happen if every form of control in the universe, in nature, within a country, school, or a family, disappeared for a single day?

Conclusions and other considerations

In the universe there is a certain order within apparent chaos. The Sun stays in place and the planets in our solar system follow their designated orbits; if not they would destroy each other and life on Earth would cease to exist.

Fines, judgments, jail, punishment, etc. represent the prickles that we need to live together as a society.

If every person was 100% responsible it would not be necessary to create 'prickles,' but we have not yet reached this level of evolution. Until we do we must think critically, working respectfully and responsibly to eliminate these 'prickles' and make the world a more friendly and pleasant place to live.

EPHEMERAL FLOWERS

⚙ Objective:

To be aware that every living thing has a lifecycle; everything lives and everything dies. Life is a great opportunity and this is why we should learn to value, respect, and admire the things that may one day be lost forever.

Narrative:

On one of his voyages to the different asteroids, The Little Prince came across a geographer compiling an exhaustive list of mountains, rivers, and stars in a huge book. The Prince wanted the geographer to include his rose, but the man replied:

"We don't record flowers. Ephemeral objects cannot be referenced."

"What does ephemeral mean?"

"Ephemeral means 'in danger of quickly disappearing.'"

When the Prince heard this he was very sad. He had realized that his flower was ephemeral and wouldn't last forever.

The Little Prince, Antoine de Saint-Exupéry

⚙ Reflecting on this narrative

- Can you find out what the word 'ephemeral' means?
- Have you ever talked about death in your family group?
- Have you ever experienced the death of a family member, friend, or pet?
- What emotions do you think we would experience if we lost someone that we love?
- Have you ever been responsible for caring for an animal or plant?
- Have you ever had a pet? What kind of animal was it?
- What did you need to do to take care of it? What did you like or not like to do?
- Could you draw all of the things that have special value in your life but may also be ephemeral?

⚙ Conclusions and other considerations

Our existence is ephemeral, as transitory as the autumn clouds. Our life is like lightning in the sky or a torrent that suddenly plunges down the side of a mountain after heavy rains.

Precisely because a flower sometimes only blooms for one day, or because we know that at some point our loved ones will die, it is as important to value life as a gift. Each person is a unique and special being that deserves our respect and care.

Let's stop prickling each other and get to know each other better, admire our differences, and learn to coexist with them!

THE HOUSE OF WORDS

Objective:

Become able to resolve our differences and conflicting positions without resorting to aggression. Work towards a peaceful outlook and improve our capacity for dialog.

Narrative:

In some Malian villages you will find a 'House of Words.' This is where the inhabitants gather to negotiate and resolve conflict. The house stands on columns made of stone or adobe and has no walls. Its only covering is a thatched roof that is so low that it is impossible to stand. To enter you must bow your head, reminding whoever does so that it is essential to be humble when communicating with others. There is no furniture in this House of Words; the villagers sit on the floor facing each other. If one of them, carried away by their anger or a particularly passionate discussion, rises brusquely to berate another, he hits his head against the ceiling.

The pain of this blow reminds them how important it is to be patient and that leaping up as a result of out-of-control emotions can only harm any ongoing dialog.

Reflecting on this narrative

- What do you think about the idea of a 'House of Words'? Do you think that it would be interesting to have a space like this in the classroom, at school, at home, or in your city?

- How do you feel when someone thinks differently to you? How would you react?

- Working as a class, try to make two lists: The first of 10 dart words and the second of 10 bridge words. Which emotions do you experience when someone uses either type of word when they are talking to you?

Conclusions and other considerations

The spoken word is a potent form of energy that we can use in favor of life and peace, or against them. Words can be like darts (that puncture, cause us to suffer, or stop us in our tracks) or bridges (that join people together, help us to grow, and also console us).

When words emerge from a pit of thoughtlessness and fear they are transformed into darts, injuring anyone who crosses their path and becoming huge emotional contaminants.

If, on the other hand, a word is born out of reflection and silence, it helps to gladden spirits, heal, unite, and console.

Peaceful communication is not an easy art but can be learned. Naturally it requires will, effort, and a great passion for life.

I AM MY RELATIONSHIPS

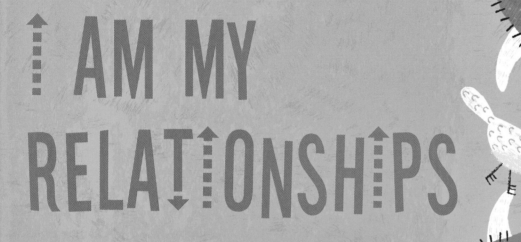

- WHAT TYPE OF RELATIONSHIPS CAN YOU IDENTIFY
    IN THE ANIMAL AND VEGETABLE KINGDOMS?
- WHAT DO THEY HOPE TO ACHIEVE?
- DID YOU KNOW THAT THERE ARE
    SIMILAR RELATIONSHIPS BETWEEN HUMANS?

There are different types of relationships between living organisms in the **natural world.** Some plants 'compete' to get the nutrients or light they need to grow. Competition only occurs if resources are limited (for example, forest plants compete for light and desert plants for scarce water resources).

Some animals compete for physical space, fighting with others when their territory is invaded. There are also animals that kill and feed on other animals: predators. Others must die so that they can live.

However, other animals and plants share resources and live in equilibrium thanks to symbiotic, commensal, or cooperative relationships. They occasionally form a wonderful cooperative relationship; insects and birds feed on plants while simultaneously ensuring their pollination and the distribution of their seeds.

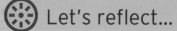 Let's reflect...

- What type of relationships have people around us formed? Are they collaborative or competitive?

- What kind of resources do you have to compete for? Do you seek recognition, affection, attention, or to be cared for? Which resource is scarce in your life?

- How do you feel when you must compete for something?

- How do you feel when you collaborate?

- How do you behave in both cases?

We are all links in a long human chain; many people came before us so that we can be here today. We are all special and unique. If we are here today it is because none of our ancestors died before they had children. No war, epidemic, accident, or illness broke the chain of life to reach us. What each of us brings to the world cannot be contributed by anyone else. Our life is a great opportunity!

We exist because many other people have made it possible. Relationships with others can help us grow, but they can also make us suffer. Humans maintain many different types of relationships in the same way that they occur in the animal and vegetable kingdoms: parasitic, symbiotic, cooperative, competitive, etc.

Let's reflect...

- Which people are helping us to grow?
- What do they do for you? What do you do for them?
- What type of person makes you suffer? Which aspects of their behavior bother you?
- Have you ever felt that anyone was persecuting you? What did you do?
- Consider your classmates. Are they collaborators or competitors? Why? How does it make you feel to perceive them in one way or the other?

43

ARE THESE RELATIONSHIPS BASED ON RESPECT **AND MUTUAL GROWTH** OR ARE THEY DESTRUCTIVE RELATIONSHIPS?

IDEAS
TO IMPROVE OUR RELATIONSHIPS

BREAK THE TWIG!

⚙ Objective:
Underline the importance of working in a team, helping each other, and a family united.

Narrative:
An old, dying man summons his family members. He gives to each one a short but sturdy twig.

"Break the twigs!" he orders.

With some effort, they break the twigs in half.

"This is what happens to a lonely soul: It breaks easily," the old man explains.

Then he gives each of his relatives another twig and announces:

"This is how I would like you to live when I am dead. Make bundles of several twigs. And now, break the bundles in half."

But none of them could break the twigs that they had bundled together. The old man looked at them, smiling:

"We are stronger when we are with other souls. If we are united, nobody will be able to break us."

⚙ Reflecting on this narrative

- What do the expressions 'union' and 'mutual help' mean to you?
- Who do you feel united to? What binds you together?
- Do you think that all families are united? Why?
- Which person in your family do you feel most united to? What kind of person are they?
- Which people have helped you through difficult times?
- Do you feel accompanied? Have you sometimes felt lonely?
- If you were a twig, which two or three other 'twigs' would you include in your bundle?

⚙ Conclusions and other considerations

We are all part of a family, biological or otherwise. A family is the group of people who support us, help us grow, and share their lives with us. As we grow we incorporate other people into our lives; we are not linked to them by blood, but by affection. They will become our 'chosen family.'

The affectionate, supportive, and unifying networks that connect us with other people can save us in difficult situations and improve our lives by filling them with light when everything is going well.

It is very important to join our twig with many others, forming an unbreakable bundle! If we are united by love, we are stronger together.

A WALL FULL OF NAMES

Objective:

Be aware that the person we are and will become is the result of teamwork and the contribution and influence of the many significant people who help us to grow.

Activity:

"Paint the names of those people that fill your life with light on a wall at home. You will never feel abandoned or alone."

Miquel Martí i Pol

Begin this activity by giving each participant an A3 sheet of paper, which they should stick to the wall.

Imagine that you had an entire wall at home at your disposal. It could be a wall in your bedroom, the hallway, or living room. Firstly, you need to decide which color you wish to paint it. You should choose a color that brings you well-being and happiness. Once this is done, take a few moments to reflect on those people that are important in your life: Those that fill you with light, have taught you important lessons, worry about you, help you to grow and become a better person, and those with whom you can freely share your thoughts, emotions, and dreams.

Now write their names on the wall using any color, text font, and letter size that you want to. Just don't forget anyone, and always leave room to add new names!

Reflecting on this exercise

- Are there a lot of names on your wall?

- Which people on the wall needed to exist so that you could be here today?

- Whose name have you written in the largest letters? Why? What have you learned from them?

- Could you write next to each name something that they have contributed to you or that illuminates your life?

- What kind of daily 'THANK YOU' would you give to each of them?

- Which people would write your name on their wall? Why?

- Have you written your own name? Why?

Conclusions and other considerations

We will meet many people as we travel along life's road. We will share some of the journey with them before they turn off at a junction or crossroads. However, there are others who will serve as referents throughout our lives, whether they are physically present or not. These are the people who we will carry forever in our hearts, and they deserve a place on our wall of 'shining names.'

Life is a great adventure. When the end comes it doesn't matter who has accumulated more wealth or gone further, but who has loved more. We hope that you are able to fill your emotional wall with the names of the many people who have loved you and whom you have been lucky enough to have loved!

THE BEST OF OTHERS

⚙ Objective:
Learn to be attentive to the values and qualities of others, instead of focusing solely on what annoys us about them.

Activity:
Stick a piece of paper to each participant's back and give them a packet of post-its.

For this activity they walk around the classroom in silence while music plays in the background. As they encounter another group member they write a personal quality or something they especially like about them on a post-it. This post-it is then attached to the sheet of paper on their back.

Each group member can attach as many post-its as positive qualities that they identify in their colleagues. It doesn't matter if someone else has already noted the same qualities.

After a while each participant removes their sheet and reads what others have written about them. They copy the comments down onto another sheet of paper, noting to one side if they recognize these qualities in themselves or not.

Finally, all participants sit in a circle to share how it felt to give and receive positive reinforcement.

⚙ Reflecting on this exercise

- What was easier: Indentifying positive qualities or what you don't like about someone?

- Why do you think that this was the case?

- Was there any person you didn't give feedback to? Why?

- Can we recognize sincerity and positive qualities in a person we don't know well?

- Which emotions did this group dynamic connect you to? Can you make an emotional scanner?

- Do you think that we express often enough what we like about others?

⚙ Conclusions and other considerations

We all have personal qualities. Sometimes we show them, while at other times we keep them hidden.

While they are not always useful, they can sometimes help us. Looking for the best in yourself and those around you is a great way to improve your relationships.

When we recognize something we like in a person, it is important that we tell them. In this we collaborate in improving our own self-esteem, nourishing our relationship with this person with emotional vitamins.

When someone acknowledges one of our qualities it is important to graciously accept and thank them for it. Favoring a person in this way means that they will continue to generously seed emotional vitamins.

I AM RESPONSIBLE FOR MY ROSE

Objective:

Reflect on the importance of looking after what we love. Learning to love is much more than simply saying "I love you"; it means taking responsibility and working towards the welfare of our loved ones.

Narrative:

The Fox and The Little Prince were talking:

"And now here is my secret, a very simple secret," said the Fox. "It is only with the heart that one can rightly see; what is essential is invisible to the eye. It's the time that you have invested in your rose that makes it so important. Humans have long since forgotten this truth, but you shouldn't. One must be held forever responsible for what they have cultivated. You are responsible for your rose."

"True," The Little Prince reflected. "My flower is more important than the others because it is the one which I have watered, protected from the wind, and kept safe from disease. I have sometimes heard it complain, or display its vanity, and even seen it wilt. It is my rose and I am responsible for my rose . . . " he repeated, so that he would always remember it.

The Little Prince, Antoine de Saint-Exupéry

Reflecting on this narrative

- What do you think that "it is only with the heart that one can rightly see" means?

- What are the essential things in our lives that we cannot see with our eyes?

- Why do you think the Fox tells The Little Prince that it is the time he has invested in his rose which has made it so important?

- What do you think you would value more: Something that takes a year to create or something that can be created in an instant? Why? Which would you find harder to destroy: The first thing or the second?

- Do you think we are responsible for what we bring into this world? Why? Are your parents responsible for you? And what are you responsible for?

- In which different ways can we care for a friend? If someone acts indifferently towards us and does not contribute to our well-being, do they truly love us?

Conclusions and other considerations

To live is always 'living with.' We are responsible for the type of person we are and the relationships we have.

'Love' is a verb. A verb means an action. In order to love someone we must give them our time, attention, and care, avoid damaging them, and make sure that they are not hurt by other people; we must nourish them with emotional vitamins and share our lives with them. Finally, we must dedicate ourselves to work towards their personal growth and well-being.

Love is the most transforming, curative, and creative emotional energy source there is. However widely it is dispersed, it never runs out. It is inexhaustible: Ecological, renewable, and sustainable.

HOW DO I KEEP A FRIEND?

✿ Objective:

Consider friendship and the conditions that it needs to grow healthily.

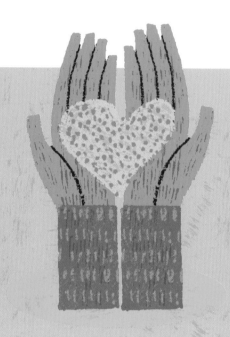

Situation:

One day a 12-year-old boy was walking along the beach with his mother. Suddenly he turned to her and determinedly asked:

"Mom, what must I do to keep a friend?"

His mother thought for a few moments before stooping down and scooping up sand with both hands. Holding both palms face-up, she clasped one of them into a fist. The sand began to slip through her fingers. The harder she squeezed, the more sand ran out onto the floor. But all this time she kept her other hand open, and the sand stayed where it was.

The boy, observing his mother's display with admiration, clearly understood her message.

✪ Reflecting on this situation

- Which important message was the mother communicating to her son?

- What was the significance of the hand that tried to retain the sand by squeezing it?

- What was the significance of the hand that remained open?

- Are there any aspects of your behavior that can suffocate friendship?

- Have you ever had the impression that someone wants to squeeze you in their fist? What emotions did you experience? How did you react?

- Have you ever demanded exclusivity in your relationship with a friend? Why?

- How do you think that we can grow in confidence within a friendly relationship?

✪ Conclusions and other considerations

Friendship requires a suitable emotional habitat in which to thrive. It needs the best of care, as if it were a delicate plant. The worst thing we can do with these types of emotions is to lock them away or tie them up. If we do this we will suffocate a friendship.

Friendship also requires freedom and respect. A friend should never be considered our property or in our possession. We have no right to exclusivity. In fact, when we want 'someone to stay' just with us, we are trying to hold them back and lock them up; this will eventually kill a relationship.

Trust must always accompany friendship. Only if we learn to respect each other's space, decisions, and right to love and be loved by other people can we hope to maintain and cultivate a friendship throughout our lives.

FOOTSTEPS ON THE PATH

Objective:

To reflect on the people who have guided us along a positive life path and learn how to identify our best referents.

Activity:

Acquire a big roll of packaging paper, which is spread across the floor of the classroom as if it were a carpet. Different-colored paints (non-toxic, as they will come in contact with skin) are poured into containers large enough to dip feet inside. Other containers holding water must also be at hand to wash feet in. You will also need some newspaper to protect the floor, and rolls of paper towels to dry up with.

Each participant chooses a color, dips their feet in the paint, and walks three steps on the paper carpet, making footprints. Next they clean their feet while another participant leaves their footprints along the path. Repeat as many times as you feel necessary.

Once the paint dries, each child writes within their own footprints the name of a person that they regard as a referent and has brought something positive to their lives. It is acceptable to use historical, religious, and political figures as well as personalities from the world of literature, ecology, etc., that they deem have done amazing things for humanity.

Once this part of the exercise is completed each participant should write a short text within their footprints giving the reasons for their choice.

Reflecting on this exercise

- What is a referent?

- Are all referents positive? Do you think that there are people who have a negative influence on those around them?

- Can you find three historical figures who have had a positive influence on the history of humanity, and three others who have had a negative influence?

- How do you think we can tell if someone is influencing us in a positive or negative way?

- What kind of footprints would you rather leave on your walk through the world?

- Which single word would you choose to write within every one of your footprints?

Conclusions and other considerations

Not every path is good to 'travel along.' Some lead nowhere and many are narrow alleyways that lead to a dead end.

If you were lost and saw a group of tracks leading in opposite directions, would you like to know which of them could best show you the way? It is important to learn to recognize the right footprints to guide our lives.

Throughout the history of humanity some people have been true referents, indicating the best direction of travel (teachers, philosophers, pacifists, poets, etc.). Their lives and messages have proven valuable routes to creating a better world.

In our personal history there are also people who point the way; some want nothing but good for us, while others may try to use us. It is important to understand how to properly identify the type of footprints they have made so that we can find the best path to follow.

SOWING
HAPPINESS

- **W**HAT WOULD YOU THINK OF A GARDENER WHO PLANTED POTATOES AND **EXPECTED ORCHIDS TO GROW?**
- **A**RE YOU SOWING THE SEEDS **OF FRUIT THAT YOU WANT TO HARVEST DURING YOUR LIFETIME?**
- **D**O YOU BELIEVE THAT BY SOWING ANGER YOU WILL **OBTAIN HAPPINESS?**

53

Did you know that there are more than 25,000 different species of orchids that have adapted to the most diverse environments on the planet? It is considered a very delicate plant but the truth is that, besides its obvious beauty, it has a great capacity to adapt. But if we want to cultivate an orchid we need to understand: What its needs are, what keeps it healthy, and what can destroy it. Only then will we be able to pamper and care for it as it deserves. For example, we should consider that it absorbs moisture through its leaves, so the best way to nourish it is to spray it with a mist of distilled water. Did you know that? Furthermore, its roots are irrigated by immersion; we must leave it in a container of water so that it can absorb however much it needs. A genuine work of art!

Like the orchid, every plant, animal, and creature that lives on Earth is different. To preserve each species we have to be aware of which habitat is better suited to its development. We only have one planet and it needs immediate and ongoing care. If we destroy our ecosystems, we will die along with them. Ecology reminds us that we are part of a 'whole'; we must intelligently use our resources so that the variety of species remains an enriching source for all of us.

Let's reflect...

- Did you know that UNESCO grants the title of Biosphere Reserve to territories that preserve ecosystem models characteristic of each of the natural world's habitats, because the unique species living within them must be protected?

- Can you find information on some of the Biosphere Reserves in your country? Which singular species inhabit them?

We also need to create protected spaces **inside ourselves** where valuable and particularly delicate feelings that need special care can prosper. There are unique emotional species such as love and happiness that can only survive in territories that are free of emotional pollution.

Do you know what brings happiness into our lives?

Experiments have been carried out with people who have won a lot of money playing the lottery. Although their levels of happiness increased to begin with, after just one year they had returned to normal. More money does not make us happier in the long-term.

Some countries such as Bhutan measure GNH (Gross National Happiness) in their inhabitants, aware that it is a more important indicator of human development than GDP (Gross Domestic Product), an economic indicator. To calculate GNH they consider the maintenance of familial relationships, the balance between body and mind, respect for the environment, and the sense of communal solidarity.

✳ Let's reflect...

- Do you know where Bhutan is? Can you find out more about this special country?

- What does the expression 'communal solidarity' mean to you? Can you find any examples?

- What can we do to maintain a suitable balance between our bodies and our minds?

55

DO YOU WANT TO HELP CREATE PROTECTED SPACES **WHERE HAPPINESS CAN GROW MORE AND MORE?**

LET'S PROPOSE A TOAST!

⊛ Objective:

Share the joy of living with others. Realize that our life is worthwhile and that there is so much that we can propose a toast to.

Activity:

On special occasions people often show their happiness by proposing a toast that celebrates what makes them feel good, or to wish those present health and long life. They are expressing their hope that good things that have already lasted a long time can improve even more.

This activity requires the group to think of:

- five personal characteristics that they like
- five people
- five happy moments
- five reasons to be happy
- five skills that they possess

Each participant writes all the reasons for which they are proposing their toast on small pieces of card. Pass around a yellow paper cup onto which the participants, silent throughout, glue their cards.

Then each participant in turn holds the cup and stands up, saying: "I propose a toast to . . . " before reading their motives in a clear, loud voice. After they have finished, the rest of the group stands and says together "we will toast to that."

When all group members have taken their turn, each one explains how it felt to participate in the toast.

⊛ Reflecting on this exercise

- On an energy scale of 1-10, how did you feel before you proposed your toast?
- On an energy scale of 1-10, how did you feel after you proposed your toast?
- Was finding so many positive things difficult or easy? Why do you think that was?
- How did you feel when your classmates proposed their toasts?
- Did the group have any motives in common for proposing a toast?

⊛ Conclusions and other considerations

Happiness does not suddenly appear, but is something that we must build with the materials that life has gifted to us: our qualities and capacities and the things that happen to us every day.

If we go about things the right way, as difficult as any situation may appear, we will be able to escape from it; we will become resilient and able to keep our inner selves intact.

Therefore happiness is not something that is bought, depends on others, or is a gift from someone else. It consists of mental, emotional, and spiritual well-being, and depends for the most part on our own personal work.

One of the ways to cultivate this emotional species is to fertilize it with joy and propose a daily toast for all that is worthwhile in our lives.

FIVE SEEDS OF HAPPINESS

⚘ Objective:

To sow gratitude as the seed of happiness, for those people who are contributing something positive to our lives.

Activity:

Hand out five different colored cards to each participant, asking them to create a drawing or collage representing happiness on each card. They should also have access to paints, felt-tip pens, pencils, glue, scissors, and magazines.

Once their five cards are ready, ask them to think of five special people who they recognize have contributed something positive to their lives and send them a thank you letter.

On the back of the card they then compose their thank you letter, citing their reasons for writing it. They must include a postscript which reads: "This card is intended to sow happiness. If you want to join in, please send your own thank you cards with this postscript to five special people in your life. Together we can improve the emotional weather!"

Once the exercise is completed the cards are placed into envelopes, stamps affixed, and mailed to the addressees.

⚘ Reflecting on this exercise

- How did you feel when you were writing the happiness cards?

- Was it easy to choose the five special people that you wanted to thank?

- How do you think that they will feel when they receive your thank you letters?

- How would you feel if you received a THANK YOU like this?

- Do you think the recipients will be encouraged to join in the sowing of happiness?

⚘ Conclusions and other considerations

Generosity is an important value, an emotional vitamin that makes happiness grow. It means knowing how to give and receive life's gifts with gratitude.

Generosity begins within ourselves. We must be aware that we are valuable and deserve to be loved and cared for. Only if we practice generosity with ourselves can we be more generous with others. Never forget that you can't give something you don't possess.

Gratitude is a seed similar to that produced by the dandelion; it can travel long distances and floats away if you blow on it. If we want to increase happiness levels in our family, friends, and society, we need to sow generosity and gratitude every day!

THE FORMULA FOR HAPPINESS

⚙ Objective:

Reflect on the meaning of the word 'happiness.' Realize that while it can mean different things to different people, certain ingredients are always present.

Activity:

Form three working groups and relate to them:

You are three teams of scientists who are competing to find the formula for happiness and win the World's Best Scientists of the Year Award.

You have one hour to reach a consensus on which 10 ingredients to use, and in what proportions they should be used to create this formula. You then have a further half an hour to write up your formula and design the package in which it will be distributed, its label, and an instruction booklet (contraindications, incompatibilities, dosage, preparation, price, etc.).

Finally, each team presents their work and answers questions from the rest of the group.

Once all of the working groups have completed their presentations, they can decide on a definitive formula containing the best ingredients from all three of them.

⚙ Reflecting on this exercise

- How many of the ingredients for your formula for happiness are available to buy?

- How many ingredients do not depend on how much money you have?

- Which ingredient was most highly valued across the three groups?

- Do you think that most of the ingredients can be acquired from yourself?

- Why do you think that there are people who feel so unhappy?

- What would your current level of happiness be, on a scale of 1–10?

- What do you think you can do to increase your level of happiness?

⚙ Conclusions and other considerations

Every person has their own way of being happy. For some, happiness is linked to health, a certain level of material well-being, or professional fulfillment; for others it is linked to inner peace, serenity, a connection with nature, and maintaining high-quality relationships with others. Others may seek freedom, culture, and a lot of love . . . what is your formula for happiness? Have you found your 10 ingredients?

'Happiness' is not the same as 'joy.' Joy is like a light that turns quickly on and off; it normally manifests itself when good things suddenly happen to us. Happiness is a more permanent feeling that does not depend so much on what happens to us as the manner in which we live.

A LETTER IN THE PARK

✿ Objective:

Recognize one's ability to bring happiness to others.

Activity:

Give each participant a worksheet with the following instructions:

You are a very sporty person and, just like every other day, you have woken up early to jog around the park in front of your home. Halfway around your circuit you come across a sealed envelope on the ground. You stop and pick it up. You are very surprised to see that it has your name written on it. This letter is for you!

Intrigued and full of curiosity, you sit on a nearby bench and open the envelope. Inside is a note written to you. You read it. It is a beautiful letter written by the person who you love and know best in the world. They are telling you everything they like about you, what makes them happy, all of the good things that you have done, what you bring to the people around you and everything that you care for and love; the letter also expresses hope that you will continue to be a person who takes happiness wherever you go.

In this activity you will be the author of such a beautiful letter.

✿ Reflecting on this exercise

- Who do you think are the people that you know best in the world? Are you absolutely sure?

- Do you consider yourself generous? What specific things do you do that make you generous?

- Which three of your qualities do you think the people who know you best would highlight?

- How did you start your letter? How did you conclude it?

- How would you feel if this had really happened to you?

- Do you think we discuss the things we like about each other often enough? What do you think would happen if we did it by letter, like this?

- Which people close to you bring happiness to your life? Can you cite three of their qualities?

✿ Conclusions and other considerations

To achieve true happiness and serenity we must ally ourselves with our minds and emotions.

The basic ingredient to be happy and to create happiness is love. If we share our love we will become more generous and better-adapted people.

It is impossible to build our happiness around others. Even if it is only for purely selfish reasons we must be concerned for and sympathize with the other living beings who share our world.

THE PLANT OF HAPPINESS

⚘ Objective:

Be aware that happiness does not suddenly appear but is something that every person must cultivate and care for throughout their lives.

Activity:

Visit a plant nursery and listen carefully as the gardeners explain how they cultivate the different varieties of plants.

At the end of the visit, after the question-and-answers session, each student should choose a young potted plant from a previously prepared selection. They then write their own names on an adhesive label before sticking it to their chosen pot.

Then they should investigate the name of the plant, its origins, characteristics, preferential habitat, how much water it requires, which vitamins it likes, with which other plants it can coexist, when it should be moved to a new pot, how it reproduces, etc., and write up an information sheet detailing all of this information.

They should also look in the nursery for a fully grown version of the same plant and photograph it.

Then distribute an instruction sheet:

From this moment onwards you must take care of your chosen plant, providing everything that it needs to flourish and grow. The sheet that you have written up, together with the photograph that you have made of a fully grown plant will help you.

The second part of the activity is then explained: Now carry out the same task, but this time carefully consider yourself. You must create an information sheet that details all of your characteristics, using the same sections as on your plant information sheet. The idea is that this will help you to 'flourish' and 'grow,' to become responsible for the 'plant' that you are.

⚙ Reflecting on this exercise

- Why did you choose your plant and not another?

- What is the most important thing to bear in mind so that your plant thrives and grows into the adult plant you have photographed?

- Which personal ingredients (qualities, values, and actions) will you have to employ to achieve this?

- How should you care for yourself to ensure that you become a balanced and happy person?

- What was the most important lesson that you learned during this exercise?

⚙ Conclusions and other considerations

Happiness is an emotion that promotes trust, serenity, joy, hope, and life-balance. It requires generosity, solidarity, and gratitude in order to prosper, but above all a great deal of wisdom and love.

As you can see, this cultivation is not easy; but if you use the right mix of ingredients it will flourish and make an inner light shine in those who have sown it.

Pain, fear, hopelessness, and hatred will try to steal our happiness. When they are present, happiness will disappear. When this happens we should remember what Helen Keller said: "When one door of happiness closes another opens, but often we look so long at the closed door that we do not see the one that has been opened for us."

HAPPINESS COCKTAIL

✺ Objective:

Reflect on the ingredients that, properly mixed, bring us happiness. Realize that each person's happiness has its own unique formula that only they can discover.

Activity:

Prepare 10 small glass jars by filling them with water. The water in each one is dyed with a different food coloring. The mentor attaches a label to each jar, on which they have written the name of an ingredient related to happiness: gratitude, sense of humor, generosity, inner peace, smiles, love, time, fun, understanding, joy, etc.

Each participant is then given a transparent glass labeled 'HAPPINESS COCKTAIL,' a large syringe (capacity 10cm^3) to use as a measure, and a spoon to mix with. Distribute notepads and pens so that each participant can record the formula for happiness

that they have chosen to create their cocktail.

The exercise involves mixing quantities of colored water from whichever jars they choose and creating a cocktail that they believe will bring them happiness. They should record the quantity of liquid from each jar that they add to their glasses. The cocktail should be mixed well, and the resulting color observed.

Then each child presents their cocktail and the formula they have discovered to the rest of the group. They should observe the diversity of hues and colors and the different quantities that each of them has used and noted.

✺ Reflecting on this exercise

- Did you use all 10 of the ingredients?

- Were there any ingredients that you didn't want to use?

- Which ingredient did you use the most of? Why?

- Have you missed any ingredients essential for you?

- What conclusions can you draw from this exercise?

✺ Conclusions and other considerations

There are many things that we can do to bring happiness into our lives:
- Allocate time to everything we do and not delay things.
- Enjoy the small things that go well.
- Admit errors and learn to use them to improve ourselves.
- Look for something positive in every situation.
- Cultivate a sense of humor and smile often.
- Help others whenever possible.
- Care for the people around us.
- Take physical exercise and learn to relax.
- Listen to music.
- Do something creative and develop our imagination.
- Learn to listen.
- Show the whole world the love that we feel. There is no single formula for happiness. Each person must mix their own cocktail and work to obtain the ingredients that make this possible.

ABOUT THE AUTHORS

Maria Mercè Conangla and **Jaume Soler** are psychologists and the founders of the *Fundació Àmbit* institute for personal development in Barcelona (Spain), a non-profit organization that has specialized in providing training, counseling, and resources for personal growth, education, and emotional management since 1996. Two of its innovative projects are the *ÀMBITuniversit@rtdelviure* program and its *Master's in Emotional Ecology*, which the authors co-direct. Their research and work in the context of humanist psychology and emotional management led them to develop a new concept of emotional ecology in 2002, which they have since advocated in eleven co-authored books. Both are lecturers and collaborating professors in a variety of master's degrees linked to emotional management, well-being, and personal growth at the University of Barcelona.

www.ecologiaemocional.org | www.fundacioambit.org

Other Schiffer Books by the Author:
Emotional Explorers: A Creative Approach to Managing Emotions,
ISBN: 978-0-7643-5553-0
Feelings Forecasters: A Creative Approach to Managing Emotions,
ISBN: 978-0-7643-5624-7

Other Schiffer Books on Related Subjects:
Unraveling Rose by Brian Wray,
ISBN: 978-0-7643-5393-2

Copyright © 2018 by Schiffer Publishing

Originally published as [Originally published as Energías y Relaciones Para Crecer by Maria Mercè Conangla and Jaume Soler Illustrations by Paloma Valdivia ©2013 ParramónPaidotribo Translated from Spanish by Ian Hayden Jones.

Library of Congress Control Number: 2018937050

Designed by: Jack Chappell
Cover Design by: Molly Shields
Editorial Direction: María Fernanda Canal
Illustrations: Paloma Valdivia
Edition: Cristina Vilella
Graphic design and layout: Alehop
Type set in: Stereofidelic/Jivetalk/ Freehand575/Interstate

ISBN: 978-0-7643-5555-4
Printed in China

Published by Schiffer Publishing, Ltd.
4880 Lower Valley Road
Atglen, PA 19310
Phone: (610) 593-1777; Fax: (610) 593-2002
E-mail: Info@schifferbooks.com
Web: www.schifferbooks.com

For our complete selection of fine books on this and related subjects, please visit our website at www.schifferbooks.com. You may also write for a free catalog.

Schiffer Publishing's titles are available at special discounts for bulk purchases for sales promotions or premiums. Special editions, including personalized covers, corporate imprints, and excerpts, can be created in large quantities for special needs. For more information, contact the publisher.

We are always looking for people to write books on new and related subjects. If you have an idea for a book, please contact us at proposals@ schifferbooks.com.